December, 1993

ONE LITTLE GOAT ~ HAD GADYA

lettered & illustrated by
BETSY PLATKIN TEUTSCH

Copyright © 1990 by Betsy Platkin Teutsch

10 9 8 7 6 5 4 3 2 1

All rights reserved.
Printed in the United States of America.
No part of this book may be used or reproduced
in any manner whatsoever without written permission
from Jason Aronson Inc. except in the case of brief quotations
in reviews for inclusion in a magazine, newspaper, or broadcast.

Library of Congress Cataloging-in-Publication Data

Had gadya. English & Aramaic.
One little goat—Had gadya / [lettered and illustrated by] Betsy
Platkin Teutsch.
p. cm.
Summary: After a little goat is eaten by a cat, troubles escalate
until the Holy One puts things right. The song is sung at the end of
the seder on Passover.
English and Aramaic.
ISBN 0-87668-824-5
1. Seder—Liturgy—Texts—Juvenile literature. 2. Judaism—
Liturgy—Texts—Juvenile literature. [1. Jews—Music.
2. Passover. 3. Songs. 4. Aramaic language materials—Bilingual.]
I. Teutsch, Betsy Platkin, ill. II. Title. III. Title: Had gadya.
BM670.H28T4813 1990
296.4'37—dc20   89-18298   CIP   AC HE

Manufactured in the United States of America.
Jason Aronson Inc. offers books and cassettes.
For information and catalog write to Jason Aronson Inc.,
230 Livingston Street,
Northvale, New Jersey 07647.

For my parents,
Fritzie and Sam Platkin

The little goat (poor him!)
That Papa bought for two zuzim.
ONE LITTLE GOAT,
ONE LITTLE GOAT!

חַד גַּדְיָא, חַד גַּדְיָא,
דְזַבַּן אַבָּא בִּתְרֵי זוּזֵי,
חַד גַּדְיָא,
חַד גַּדְיָא!

Then came a cat
And ate the little goat (poor him!)
That Papa bought for two zuzim.
ONE LITTLE GOAT,
ONE LITTLE GOAT!

וְאָתָא שׁוּנְרָא
וְאָכַל לְגַדְיָא
דְזַבַן אַבָּא בִּתְרֵי זוּזֵי
חַד גַּדְיָא,
חַד גַּדְיָא!

Then came a dog
And bit the cat
That ate the little goat (poor him!)
That Papa bought for two zuzim.
ONE LITTLE GOAT,
ONE LITTLE GOAT!

וְאָתָא כַלְבָּא
וְנָשַׁךְ לְשׁוּנְרָא
דְאָכַל לְגַדְיָא
דְזַבַּן אַבָּא בִּתְרֵי זוּזֵי
חַד גַּדְיָא,
חַד גַּדְיָא!

Then came a stick

And beat the dog

That bit the cat

That ate the little goat (poor him!)

That Papa bought for two zuzim.

ONE LITTLE GOAT,

ONE LITTLE GOAT!

וְאָתָא חוּטְרָא
וְהִכָּה לְכַלְבָּא
דְנָשַׁךְ לְשׁוּנְרָא
דְאָכַל לְגַדְיָא
דְזַבֵּן אַבָּא בִּתְרֵי זוּזֵי
חַד גַּדְיָא,
חַד גַּדְיָא!

Then came a fire
And burned the stick
That beat the dog
That bit the cat
That ate the little goat (poor him!)
That Papa bought for two zuzim.
ONE LITTLE GOAT,
ONE LITTLE GOAT !

וְאָתָא נוּרָא
וְשָׂרַף לְחוּטְרָא
דְהִכָּה לְכַלְבָּא
דְנָשַׁךְ לְשׁוּנְרָא
דְאָכַל לְגַדְיָא
דְזָבַן אַבָּא בִּתְרֵי זוּזֵי
חַד גַּדְיָא,
חַד גַּדְיָא !

Then came the water
And quenched the fire
That burned the stick
That beat the dog
That bit the cat
That ate the little goat (poor him!)
That Papa bought for two zuzim.
ONE LITTLE GOAT,
ONE LITTLE GOAT!

וְאָתָא מַיָּא
וְכָבָה לְנוּרָא
דְשָׂרַף לְחוּטְרָא
דְהִכָּה לְכַלְבָּא
דְנָשַׁךְ לְשׁוּנְרָא
דְאָכַל לְגַדְיָא
דְזַבַּן אַבָּא בִּתְרֵי זוּזֵי
חַד גַּדְיָא, חַד גַּדְיָא !

Then came an ox
And drank the water
That quenched the fire
That burned the stick
That beat the dog
That bit the cat
That ate the little goat (poor him!)
That Papa bought for two zuzim.
ONE LITTLE GOAT,
ONE LITTLE GOAT!

וְאָתָא תּוֹרָא
וְשָׁתָה לְמַיָּא
דְּכָבָה לְנוּרָא
דְּשָׂרַף לְחוּטְרָא
דְּהִכָּה לְכַלְבָּא
דְּנָשַׁךְ לְשׁוּנְרָא
דְּאָכַל לְגַדְיָא
דְּזַבַּן אַבָּא בִּתְרֵי זוּזֵי
חַד גַּדְיָא,
חַד גַּדְיָא!

Then came a butcher

And killed the ox

That drank the water

That quenched the fire

That burned the stick

That beat the dog

That bit the cat

That ate the little goat (poor him!)

That Papa bought for two zuzim.

ONE LITTLE GOAT,

ONE LITTLE GOAT!

וְאָתָא הַשּׁוֹחֵט

וְשָׁחַט לְתוֹרָא

דְּשָׁתָה לְמַיָּא

דְּכָבָה לְנוּרָא

דְּשָׂרַף לְחוּטְרָא

דְּהִכָּה לְכַלְבָּא

דְּנָשַׁךְ לְשׁוּנְרָא

דְּאָכַל לְגַדְיָא

דְּזַבֵּן אַבָּא בִּתְרֵי זוּזֵי

חַד גַּדְיָא,

חַד גַּדְיָא!

Then came the angel of death
And slew the butcher
That killed the ox
That drank the water
That quenched the fire
That burned the stick
That beat the dog
That bit the cat
That ate the little goat (poor him!)
That Papa bought for two zuzim.
ONE LITTLE GOAT,
ONE LITTLE GOAT!

וְאָתָא מַלְאַךְ הַמָּוֶת
וְשָׁחַט לְשׁוֹחֵט
דְּשָׁחַט לְתוֹרָא
דְּשָׁתָה לְמַיָּא
דְּכָבָה לְנוּרָא
דְּשָׂרַף לְחוּטְרָא
דְּהִכָּה לְכַלְבָּא
דְּנָשַׁךְ לְשׁוּנְרָא
דְּאָכַל לְגַדְיָא
דְּזַבֵּן אַבָּא בִּתְרֵי זוּזֵי
חַד גַּדְיָא,
חַד גַּדְיָא !

Then came The Holy One of Blessing	וְאָתָא הַקָּדוֹשׁ בָּרוּךְ הוּא
And killed the angel of death	וְשָׁחַט לְמַלְאַךְ הַמָּוֶת
That slew the butcher	דְּשָׁחַט לְשׁוֹחֵט
That killed the ox	דְּשָׁחַט לְתוֹרָא
That drank the water	דְּשָׁתָה לְמַיָּא
That quenched the fire	דְּכָבָה לְנוּרָא
That burned the stick	דְּשָׂרַף לְחוּטְרָא
That beat the dog	דְּהִכָּה לְכַלְבָּא
That bit the cat	דְּנָשַׁךְ לְשׁוּנְרָא
That ate the little goat (poor him!)	דְּאָכַל לְגַדְיָא
That Papa bought for two zuzim.	דְּזַבִּן אַבָּא בִּתְרֵי זוּזֵי

ONE LITTLE GOAT,   **חַד גַּדְיָא,**
ONE LITTLE GOAT!   **חַד גַּדְיָא!**

Why is Had Gadya part of the Haggadah? And who is the little goat?

Had Gadya is a folk song intended to interest and amuse children at the Seder. (You may have heard of similar nursery rhymes such as <u>The House that Jack Built</u>.) Had Gadya is over 400 years old, and throughout the generations Jewish children - and adults, too - have enjoyed singing it. Some families like to see who can sing it the fastest without making a mistake.

No one knows for sure who the little goat is, but Jewish scholars from the past have had ideas about him. They think he stands for the Jewish people. Though there have been many enemies who have tried to destroy Israel, each one in turn has been destroyed. God alone triumphs.

One commentator even suggested who is included in Had Gadya:

The cat = the Assyrians
　　The dog = the Babylonians
　　　　The stick = the Persians
　　　　　　The water = the Macedonians
　　　　　　　　The water = the Romans
　　　　　　　　　　The ox = the Saracens
　　　　　　　　　　　　The butcher = the Crusaders
　　　　　　　　　　　　　　The angel of death = the Ottomans

All these peoples have disappeared, but the Jewish people is still around!

Had Gadya is written in Aramaic, a language related to Hebrew and written in the same letters. Some Aramaic vocabulary is different from Hebrew, though, which is why you may have found Had Gadya hard to understand. Here's some help:

ENGLISH	HEBREW	ARAMAIC
1. one	אֶחָד	חַד
2. kid, young goat	גְּדִי	גַּדְיָא
3. that	...שֶׁ	...דְּ
4. bought	קָנָה	זְבַן
5. father	אָב	אַבָּא
6. with	בְּ...	בְּ...
7. two	שְׁתֵּי	תְּרֵי
8. zuzim (small coins)	זוּזִים	זוּזֵי
9. and	וְ...	וְ...
10. came	בָּא	אֲתָא
11. —	לְ...	לְ...
12. cat (wildcat)	חָתוּל	שׁוּנְרָא

ENGLISH	HEBREW	ARAMAIC
13. ate	אָכַל	אֲכַל
14. dog	כֶּלֶב	כַּלְבָּא
15. bit	נָשַׁךְ	נְשַׁךְ
16. stick	מַטֶּה	חוּטְרָא
17. hit	הִכָּה	הִכָּה
18. fire	אֵשׁ	נוּרָא
19. burn	שָׂרַף	שְׂרַף
20. water	מַיִם	מַיָּא
21. quench, put out	כָּבָה	כָּבָה
22. ox	שׁוֹר	תּוֹרָא
23. drink	שָׁתָה	שָׁתָה
24. butcher	שׁוֹחֵט	שׁוֹחֵט
25. slaughtered	שָׁחַט	שָׁחַט
26. angel of death	מַלְאַךְ הַמָּוֶת	מַלְאַךְ הַמָּוֶת
27. God (lit. "the Holy One Blessed be He")	הַקָּדוֹשׁ בָּרוּךְ הוּא	הַקָּדוֹשׁ בָּרוּךְ הוּא

HAD GADYA

5. V'-atah nu-rah v'sa-raf l'ḥu-trah.
   d'hi-kah l'ḥal-bah d'na-shaḥ l'shun-rah,
   d'a-ḥal l'gad-ya di-z'van a-bah bit-rei zuzei . . .

6. V'-atah ma-yah v'ḥa-vah l'nu-rah,
   d'sa-raf l'ḥu-trah d'hi-kah l'ḥal-bah,
   d'na-shaḥ l'shun-rah d'a-ḥal l'gad-ya
   di-z'van a-bah bit-rei zuzei . . .

7. V'-atah to-rah v'sha-tah l'ma-yah,
   d'ḥa-vah l'nu-rah d'sa-raf l'ḥu-trah,
   d'hi-kah l'ḥal-bah d'na-shaḥ l'shun-rah,
   d'a-ḥal l'gad-ya di-z'van a-bah bit-rei zuzei . . .

8. V'-atah ha-sho-ḥeit v'sha-ḥat l'to-rah,
   d'sha-tah l'ma-yah d'ḥa-vah l'nu-rah,
   d'sa-raf l'ḥu-trah, d'hi-kah l'ḥal-bah,
   d'na-shaḥ l'shun-rah d'a-ḥal l'gad-ya,
   di-z'van a-bah bit-rei zuzei . . .

9. V'-atah mal-aḥ ha-ma-vet v'sha-ḥat la-sho-ḥeit,
   d'sha-ḥat l'to-rah d'sha-tah l'ma-yah,
   d'ḥa-vah l'nu-rah d'sa-raf l'ḥu-trah,
   d'hi-kah l'ḥal-bah d'na-shaḥ l'shun-rah,
   d'a-ḥal l'gad-ya di-z'van a-bah bit-rei zuzei . . .

Reprinted with the permission of the CCAR.